One afternoon, Billy Rabbit fell asleep. When he woke up, it was dark and the jungle was full of strange and frightening things.

British Library Cataloguing in Publication Data
Grace, John
    It's dark!
    I. Title   II. Trotter, Stuart   III. Series
    823.914[J]
    ISBN 0-7214-1432-X

First edition

Published by Ladybird Books Ltd Loughborough Leicestershire UK
Ladybird Books Inc Auburn Maine 04210 USA

Printed in England (3)

BiG HUG
It's Dark!

by JOHN GRACE
illustrated by STUART TROTTER

Ladybird Books

One hot afternoon,
Billy Rabbit went
to sleep in the shade
of a banana leaf.

When Billy woke up the sun had gone away and the sky was full of stars.

"It's dark," said Billy.

He decided to explore the island.

"Come back, Billy," called the owl. "It's your bedtime!"

"But I'm not tired," said Billy.

Billy was excited.
He had never been
out at night before.

The jungle looked
different.

The jungle was dark
and still.

Billy was lost.

"I don't like the dark," said Billy. He was frightened.

The wind blew.
The bushes moved.
The trees shook.
Billy ran as fast as he could.

Billy hid in a cave. He heard a noise. "Snnnggrrr!"

Billy Rabbit ran away.

He ran away as fast as he could.

"Help!" he shouted.

"Hello, Billy," said Big Hug. "You're up late."

"I don't like the dark," said Billy.

"Come with me," said Big Hug.

Big Hug and Billy went into the jungle.

"The shadow you saw was made by Mozzle the hedgehog," said Big Hug.

"And the noise you heard was Old Puma snoring."

"Snnnggrrr!" went the puma.

"Who was watching me?" asked Billy.

"We were," said Hector Frog. "Frogs come out to sing at night."

The frogs sang a song for Billy.

"Snnnggrrr!" went the puma.

"Some animals go to sleep when it gets dark," yawned Billy.

"And some animals wake up," said Big Hug.

"The night-time is a special time," said Big Hug.

"Snnnggrrr!" went Billy Rabbit.